Mr. Granite Is from Another planet!

Dan Gutman

Pictures by
Jim Paillot

HarperTrophy®

An Imprint of HarperCollinsPublishers

To Emma

Mr. Granite Is from Another Planet!

Text copyright © 2008 by Dan Gutman

Illustrations copyright © 2008 by Jim Paillot

Library of Congress Cataloging-in-Publication Data is available.
ISBN 978-0-06-134611-8 (pbk.) — ISBN 978-0-06-134612-5 (lib. bdg.)

Typography by Joel Tippie

❖

First Edition

Contents

The Boringest Store in the World

My name is A.J. and I hate school.

Do you know which months are the best months of the year? July and August, of course! Because there's no school over the summer.

YAY!

The only problem is that now it's September.

BOO!

Bummer after the summer!

School starts tomorrow. So my mom said we had to go to this store called Staples to buy back-to-school supplies. Ugh! Staples is the boringest store in the history of the world. They don't sell video games or toys or any cool stuff. They just sell pens and pencils and ultraboring junk like that.

My mom had a list of things I had to get for third grade. After we found the boring book covers, boring binders, boring colored pencils, and boring glue sticks, I wanted to get a pen with a laser beam in it. Laser beams are cool. I saw this movie where they used a laser beam to kill aliens from outer space. But they don't sell pens like that at Staples.

They do have *one* cool thing—a copy machine. Copy machines are cool because you can put your head on the glass and make a funny picture of your face. It only costs eight cents! But you have to be sure to close your eyes or you'll go blind.

I stuck my head in the copy machine and closed my eyes. I was reaching for the START button when I heard the most horrible sound in the history of the world. . . .

"Hi, Arlo!"

Ugh! It was Andrea Young, this annoying girl in my class with curly brown hair. I hate her. Andrea calls me by my real

name because she knows I don't like it.

I took my head off of the copy machine. Andrea was with her mom, who looks just like Andrea but with wrinkles.

"Are you buying back-to-school supplies *too*, Arlo?" Andrea asked.

"No," I told her. "I'm skydiving."

When somebody asks you a dumb question, you should always give them a dumb answer. That's the first rule of being a kid.

"I would *never* put *my* face in a copy machine," said Andrea.

"Why not?"

"Because I'm one of a kind!" Andrea said.

"You should put your face in a paper shredder instead," I suggested.

Andrea rolled her eyes. Why can't a copy machine fall on her head?

My mom and Andrea's mom were talking about the weather. Grown-ups are really interested in weather. Nobody knows why.

So I was forced to talk to Andrea.

"Which do you like better, Arlo," Andrea asked, "this notebook with a picture of kittens on it or this one with elephants on it?"

"Do they have a notebook with a picture of elephants stomping on kittens?" I asked.

Andrea rolled her eyes again. Our moms said we could play around on the office chairs for a few minutes while they talked about the weather.

"Let's pretend we're grown-ups working in a real office!" Andrea said.

I sat at one of the desks and picked up a fake telephone.

"Send over a million dollars!" I barked into the phone. "NOW!"

"Where's my coffee?" Andrea shouted. "I'll *die* if I don't have coffee!"

"You're fired!" I barked again. "Get out!"

Pretending to be a grown-up is fun.

"I need to file some reports," Andrea said, and she rolled her chair over to a big filing cabinet. When she pulled it open, the most amazing thing in the history of the world happened.

A head popped out!

"G'day, mates!" the head said.

"AHHHHHHHHHHHH!" we screamed.

It was Mr. Granite, our new, third-grade teacher!

We Want Chocolate Cake

The first day of school is the worst day of the year. But the nice thing is that third graders are allowed to ride their bikes to school. I rode with my friends Ryan and Michael.

After we locked our bikes to the bike rack, we were told to go to the all-purpose room for an assembly. The teachers were sitting on the stage, and they were all wearing green T-shirts that said "P.A.L." on them. Mr. Klutz, our principal, was up there too. He has no hair at all. I mean *none*. Mr. Klutz was wearing a green shirt, too, and his *head* was even painted green. Mr. Klutz is nuts.

"Is it St. Patrick's Day?" I asked Neil Crouch, who we call the nude kid even though he wears clothes.

"St. Patrick's Day is in March, dumb-head," said Neil.

"So is your face," I replied.

After we finished pledging the allegiance, Mr. Klutz went to the microphone.

"Welcome back to Ella Mentry School," he announced. "I want to introduce the new members of our staff. This is Mrs. Jafee, our vice principal. And this is Mr. Brad, our school counselor. And over here is our new third-grade teacher, Mr. Granite."

The three of them stood up. Everybody clapped. I waved to Mr. Granite. I knew he was going to be my third-grade teacher because I'd met him on the beach over the summer. I even saw him yesterday at Staples.

"We're wearing green today to show that Ella Mentry School cares about the environment," said Mr. Klutz. "This year we're going to use less energy, create less waste, and help the planet. The program will be under Mr. Granite's supervision."

"Wow," I whispered to Ryan. "Mr. Granite has super vision! That means he can see through walls!"

"You returning students know I like to challenge you," Mr. Klutz continued. "So here's a new challenge. If Ella Mentry School is named the greenest school in the county for the month of September, we'll have an all-you-can-eat chocolate cake party!"

YAY!

Everybody went crazy, because we all love chocolate cake. That's the first rule of being a kid.

3

Pedal Power

After the assembly Mr. Granite led us to our new classroom. There were posters all over the walls with pictures of rocket ships and stars and planets. It was cool. But the weird thing was, instead of desks, the room was filled with exercise bicycles!

"Why are there bikes in here?" asked

this annoying girl named Emily, who is Andrea's crybaby friend.

"It's part of my new P.A.L. program," said Mr. Granite. "Pedal And Learn. Instead of burning coal or oil to get electricity to run our school, we're going to pedal these exercise bikes. So we'll learn new things, save energy, and get exercise all at the same time. It's a win-win!"

We get to ride bikes in school? Cool! Bikes are fun. I have a trick bike at home.

I hopped on a bike between Michael and Ryan.

"In third grade we're going to learn a lot about space," Mr. Granite told us. "So start pedaling, P.A.L.s!"

"I know a poem about space," I said as I started to pedal my bike. Mr. Granite said I could recite it. It goes like this:

Boys go to Mars to get candy bars.
Girls go to Jupiter to get more stupider.

"That's not nice, Arlo!" said Andrea.

"Neither is your face."

As we pedaled our bikes, Mr. Granite told us lots of stuff about the planets and stars. Did you know that Venus is the hottest planet? It can get up to nine hundred degrees there! I hope they have a lot of swimming pools on Venus. Because when I get really hot, I want to jump in a pool.

Hi
Shorty!

Did you know that
a day on Jupiter is less than
ten hours long?

Did you know that astronauts are a little
taller in space because there's no gravity
to push their bones together?

Did you know that the ancient Greeks
called our galaxy the Milky Way because

they thought it was made of drops of milk?

Those Greeks were weird.

"It takes eight minutes for the sun's light to reach Earth," Mr. Granite told us. "So if the sun exploded right now, we would still have eight minutes to live."

Emily jumped off her bike and started freaking out.

"Eight minutes to live?" she yelled. "We've got to *do* something!" Then she went running out of the room.

Emily is weird.

"At night," Mr. Granite told us, "you can see over a thousand stars with your naked eye."*

* But if you ask me, it makes no sense because we don't wear clothes on our eyes anyway.

Everybody started giggling because Mr. Granite said the word "naked." Any time anybody says "naked," you have to giggle. That's the first rule of being a kid.

"Now," Mr. Granite said, "let's learn about Uranus. . . ."

Everybody giggled again. It's hard to learn stuff when your teacher keeps saying words like "naked" and "Uranus."

After a while my legs started to feel tired. Riding a bike isn't nearly as much fun when you're just staying in one place and learning stuff. I started to pedal slower.

That's when something weird happened. The lights went out. Suddenly, the class was dark.

"EEEEEEEEKKKK!" screamed all the girls, as if they'd never been in the dark before.

"Who turned out the lights?" Michael asked.

"YOU did!" said Mr. Granite. "You need to pedal faster!"

We all started pedaling faster, and the lights went back on.

"Keep pedaling!" shouted Mr. Granite.

I thought I was gonna die!

Going Green

Boy, Mr. Granite wasn't kidding about making Ella Mentry School green. Everybody was doing their part to save energy and help the environment.

Miss Lazar, our school custodian, put solar panels up on the roof to collect the sun's rays and turn them into electricity.

Miss Lazar is bizarre!

Ms. Hannah, our art teacher, hates throwing stuff away. She told us to bring in plastic bags from home instead of throwing them in the garbage. She showed us how to make plastic bags into butterflies, kites, and dream catchers. Ms. Hannah is bananas!

Mr. Docker, our science teacher, is off his rocker. He has a car that runs on potatoes instead of gas. Mr. Docker converted the school bus to run on potatoes, too. And he helped Mrs. Yonkers, our computer teacher, to hook up potatoes to power the school computers. So now she says that "PC" stands for "potato computer." Mrs.

Yonkers is bonkers!

Mrs. Cooney, our school nurse, brought a giant tube of toothpaste to school one day. It was about the size of a first grader! Mrs. Cooney is loony! She said that when you buy large sizes of stuff, you don't have to go shopping so often. There's less waste, and you save money, too.

Ms. LaGrange, our lunch lady, told us to pack our lunches in reusable containers instead of in paper bags so we'd have less garbage. She also brought in a bunch of cows to graze on the grass in the field behind the school. Now the lawn doesn't need to be mowed anymore. And we get free milk, too!

I don't know where Ms. LaGrange got the cows. I guess she went to Rent-A-Cow. You can rent anything. Ms. LaGrange is strange.

Mrs. Roopy, our librarian, read us a book about how trees give off oxygen (which is good stuff) and absorb carbon dioxide (which is bad stuff). Then she helped us plant a tree in the middle of the library. Mrs. Roopy is loopy!

And Mr. Klutz, well, he put up a giant windmill in the field behind the school. When the wind turns the blades of the windmill, it makes electricity.

The whole school was going green! Part of the reason was that we all knew it was good to save energy and reduce waste. The other part was that we all like chocolate cake.

"Do any of you have *other* ideas to help the environment?" Mr. Granite asked us while we were pedaling to nowhere.

Little Miss I-Know-Everything was waving her hand in the air like she was trying to signal a boat across the ocean. But Mr. Granite called on me instead. So nah-nah-nah boo-boo on Andrea.

"I know a way to save energy," I said. "You should close the school down and let us stay home all day. Then we could sit around and do nothing. That would save a lot of energy."

Everybody laughed even though I didn't say anything funny.

"How about you, Andrea?" asked Mr. Granite. "Can *you* think of another way we can help the environment?"

"We could use both sides of every scrap of paper," Andrea said. "And then we could recycle it."

"That's an excellent idea, Andrea!" said Mr. Granite.

Andrea stuck out her tongue at me. What is her problem?

"Oh, snap!" whispered Ryan. "Andrea stuck her tongue out at you, A.J. Are you gonna take that?"

"At Andrea's house," I told the class,

"they use both sides of the toilet paper . . . and then they recycle it!"

"That's gross, Arlo!" Andrea said.

"So is your face," I told her.

"Oh, snap!" said Ryan.

Goo-Goo Gah-Gah

We were just about to get on our exercise bikes the next morning when the school secretary, Mrs. Patty, made an announcement over the intercom.

"Teachers, please do not throw your teacups around the teachers' lounge. Thank you."

That was weird.

"Okay, P.A.L.s," said Mr. Granite, "it's time for language arts. So start pedaling!"

We all started pedaling. But we didn't learn anything about language arts. Because you'll never believe in a million hundred years who walked into the door at that very moment!

Nobody! Because if you walked into a door, it would hurt. But you'll never believe who walked into the door*way*.

It was our old teacher, Mrs. Daisy! She was with her husband, Mr. Macky, who is our reading teacher. We hadn't seen Mrs. Daisy since we graduated from second grade in June.

"Mrs. Daisy!" we all shouted.

"Mrs. Daisy," said Mr. Granite, "to what do we owe the pleasure of your company?"

That's grown-up talk for "What are *you* doing here?"

"I missed my kids," she replied.

"We missed you too!" said Andrea, the big brownnoser.

Mrs. Daisy was holding something in her arms, but we couldn't see what it was because it was wrapped up in a pink blanket.

"Did you bring us a present?" I asked.

"Not exactly . . . ," said Mr. Macky.

"It's a *baby*, dumbhead!" shouted Andrea. "Mrs. Daisy had her baby!"

All the girls rushed over to look, as if having a baby is a big deal.

"What's her name?" Andrea asked.

"Jackie," said Mrs. Daisy. "Jackie Macky."

"What a lovely name!" Emily said. "She's beautiful!"

"She's adorable!" Andrea said.

"She stinks," I said, holding my nose.

"I think Jackie just pooped," said Mr. Macky. "We'll change her diaper in a minute."

I wasn't gonna go *near* that thing, especially after it pooped. But all the girls were coochie-coochie-cooing and saying "Goo-goo gah-gah" to Jackie Macky. All babies say "Goo-goo gah-gah." Nobody knows why. It must be the first rule of being a baby.

"I think Jackie looks just like *you,* Mrs.

Daisy!" said Emily.

"No," said Andrea. "I think Jackie looks just like *you*, Mr. Macky."

"I think she looks just like Mr. Klutz," I said. "She's as bald as a balloon."

"Arlo, that's mean!" said Andrea.

Well, it was true! All babies look alike anyway.

Jackie Macky started drooling, and then she started blowing spit bubbles. Then she put her foot in her mouth and started sucking on her toes. I thought it was pretty disgusting, but the girls thought it was cute. I know that if *I* started drooling in school, blowing spit bubbles, and sucking on my toes, nobody would think it was cute. I would probably get kicked out of school.

"WAAAA!" Jackie Macky cried. "WAAAA!"

"I think she bit her own foot," I said.

"Jackie might be pooping some more," said Mrs. Daisy. "We'd better go now."

Babies are weird.

6

English Is Weird

"Okay, everyone, back on your bikes," Mr. Granite said. "It's time for language arts."

Ugh! I hate language arts. Language is boring. Art is boring. So there's nothing more boring than language arts. Except maybe math. Math is *really* boring.

"There are some things I don't understand about the English language," Mr. Granite told us.

"Like what?" asked Andrea.

Little Miss Know-It-All keeps a dictionary on her desk so she can show everybody how smart she is.

"Why is it that noses run and feet smell?" Mr. Granite replied. "Shouldn't it be the other way around?"

"What do you mean?" asked Emily.

"Well, it seems to me that feet should run and noses should smell," Mr. Granite said. "So why do people say noses run and feet smell?"

"It's just an expression," said Michael.

"It makes no sense," said Ryan.

"My feet don't smell," I said.

"They do too, A.J.," said Neil the nude kid. "When you had that sleepover at your house, I had to sleep with your feet in my face."

"A nose would run if it had legs," Michael said.

"Feet could smell if they had a nose," said Ryan.

"Yeah, if you had a nose attached to your foot, your foot could smell," I pointed out.

"Arlo, you're just trying to get out of doing math next period," said Andrea.

"I am not."

"Are too."

We went back and forth like that for a while until Mr. Granite told us to knock it off.

"Why are there no eggs in an eggplant?" he asked the class. "And why is there no ham in a hamburger? Hot dogs aren't made from dogs. And a pineapple doesn't have apples in it. Or pine, for that matter."

"Mr. Granite is right!" said Ryan.

"English is weird," I said.

"Why are boxing rings square?" asked Mr. Granite. "If they're rings, they should be round."

"Yeah!" some of the kids agreed.

"If one tooth and another tooth are called teeth," said Mr. Granite, "and one goose and another goose are called geese, then why aren't one moose and another moose called meese?"

"Yeah!" Neil said. "What's up with that?"

"Why do we play at a recital and recite at a play?" asked Mr. Granite. "When a house burns up, how can it also burn down? And why do we drive on the parkway and park on the driveway?"

"Yeah!" everybody shouted.

"Mr. Granite is right!" I said. "The English language is messed up. If you ask me, we should complain."

"Who are you going to complain to, Arlo?" asked Andrea.

"The president!" I said. "We should write a letter to the president of the United States!"

Andrea rolled her eyes, but Mr. Granite said that writing a friendly letter to the president was a great idea. So nah-nah-nah boo-boo on Andrea.

Mr. Granite passed out paper to everybody. It's hard to write while you're riding a bike. So I kept my letter short and sweet:

Dear Mr. President,

I am a third-grade student at Ella Mentry School. I don't think it's fair that your feet smell. Do you have a nose attached to your foot?

Sincerely,
A.J.

Mr. Granite Goes Overboard

It was recess. We were on the swings in the playground. Me and the guys were talking about important stuff, like who won the big game last night. Andrea and her friends were talking about girlie stuff, like what color they should paint their toenails.

That's when Mr. Granite came over. He was carrying some kind of machine.

"Everybody off the swings!" he shouted.

"Why?" we all asked.

"I need to attach this generator to the top of the swing set," Mr. Granite replied. "So every time you swing back and forth, you'll be making electricity."

We had to get off the swing set and go over to the field near the cows and the windmill.

"I miss Mrs. Daisy," said Neil the nude kid. "She was normal."

"We used to say Mrs. Daisy was weird," Michael said. "But Mr. Granite is even weirder."

"MOOOOOOOOOO," said a cow.

"Mr. Granite is going overboard with this green stuff," said Ryan.

"He's falling out of a boat?" I asked.

"No, dumbhead," said Ryan. "I mean he's getting carried away."

"I don't see anybody carrying him away," I pointed out. I looked around to make sure nobody was carrying Mr. Granite away.

"MOOOOOOOOOO," said a cow.

"I heard that Mr. Granite is working on a machine that makes electricity every time you blink your eyes," Michael told us. "We'll have to wear it like a pair of glasses."

"That's crazy!" I said.

"I heard that Mr. Granite asked the music teacher, Mr. Loring, to write a song with just one note in it," said Neil the nude kid.

"Why?" we all asked.

"So he wouldn't waste any notes," Neil said.

"That will be the most boring song in the history of the world," I said.

"MOOOOOOOOOO," agreed a cow.

Andrea and her friends were sitting on a bench a few feet away, looking all worried.

"What's eating you?" I asked Andrea. "Did you get an A-minus on the math quiz?"

"No, Arlo," Andrea replied. "I got an A-*plus*. But I just figured something out."

"What?" we all asked.

"Maybe Mr. Granite isn't a real teacher at all," Andrea said. "Did you ever think of that?"

"What do you mean?" I asked.

"Maybe he's just *pretending* to be a

48

teacher," she said. "I think that Mr. Granite . . . is from another planet!"

"That's nuts!" I told her.

"Think about it, Arlo!" Andrea said. "Mr. Granite knows a lot about planets and stars and space, right?"

"Yeah."

"And he doesn't understand the English language very well, right?"

"Yeah."

"He has super vision too," added Neil. "He can see through walls."

"Did you ever notice that Mr. Granite doesn't have any hair growing out of his ears or nose?" Ryan asked.

Andrea might be right! After all, the first

rule of being a grown-up is that you have hair growing out of your ears and nose. My dad has to trim his nosehair every week.

Maybe Mr. Granite *is* from another planet!

"MOOOOOOOOOO," said a cow.

"He doesn't *look* like an alien," said Michael. "Aliens are little green guys with big heads."

"Maybe Mr. Granite is *disguised* as a human," I suggested.

"Yeah," said Ryan. "Maybe if we peeled off his human mask, underneath we'd find a little green guy with a big head."

"Mr. Granite is nice," Emily said. "Maybe

he's a *good* alien."

"Yeah, like E.T.," said Ryan. "That's my favorite movie. Maybe Mr. Granite is a nice alien who was left here on Earth like E.T."

"There are no *nice* aliens!" Neil said. "You're supposed to *kill* aliens."

"Yeah," I added, "with laser beams."

"Stop trying to scare Emily," said Andrea.

"Mr. Granite is probably going to take over the world and turn us into flesh-eating robots," I said.

"We've got to *do* something!" said Emily, and she went running away.

The only problem was that Emily ran

right into a cow. She was on the ground, freaking out. What a crybaby!

"MOOOOOOOOOO," said the cow.*

"OOOOOOOOOW!" said Emily, which is MOOOOOOOOO upside-down and backward.

"My dad is a policeman," said Michael, "and he says you can't accuse people of stuff unless you have proof."

"So let's get *proof* that Mr. Granite is an alien," said Neil the nude kid.

"How are we gonna get proof?" Ryan asked.

"I have an idea," Andrea told every-

---

*"MOOOOOOOOOO" is all cows know how to say. That's why cows hardly ever make phone calls.

body. "Let's follow Mr. Granite home after school. I have my camera in my backpack. We can snoop around. I'll take pictures of him when he peels off his human mask, and we'll have proof!"

Everybody agreed that Andrea was a genius and that she should get the No Bell Prize. That's a prize they give out to people who don't have bells.

The World's Biggest iPod

All afternoon I was watching Mr. Granite very carefully to see if his face was going to come off. Finally, three o'clock came and the bell rang.

"Any questions?" Mr. Granite said as we got our stuff out of our cubbies.

"Are you going to destroy our planet?"

I asked.

"Will you peel off your face?" Neil asked.

"Don't be silly," replied Mr. Granite.

Once we got outside, me, Michael, and Ryan raced to the bike rack. Andrea and Emily were already there.

"How will we find out where Mr. Granite lives?" asked Emily.

"We should drop pieces of candy on the ground," said Ryan. "That's what the boy did in *E.T.*"

"I'm not wasting my candy," I said.

"We should stalk Mr. Granite," suggested Michael.

"You mean we should hit him with

celery?" I asked. "What good would that do?"

"No, dumbhead!" said Andrea. "Stalking is—"

She never got the chance to finish her sentence, because at that very second Mr. Granite zoomed past us on his bike.

"Look!" said Ryan. "There he goes!"

We all hopped on our bikes and followed Mr. Granite, being careful not to let him see us.

"Maybe Mr. Granite will make our bikes fly," said Ryan. "That's what E.T. did."

"Will you forget about E.T. already?" Michael told Ryan.

Finally, Mr. Granite turned into a driveway. Well, I don't mean he *became* a drive-way. That would be weird. He just rode his bike up into a driveway next to a house. There was a big white box in front of the garage. It had the word "PODS" on it.

"Hey, check it out!" I told everybody. "Look at the size of that iPod!"

"Mr. Granite lives in an iPod?" asked Michael.

"Man!" I said. "How many songs do you think will fit on *that* iPod?"

"It's not an iPod, dumbheads," said Andrea. "It's one of those big storage boxes. It says PODS."

Oh.

It made sense that Mr. Granite lived in a pod. I saw this movie called *Invasion of the Body Snatchers*. It had these pod people who look just like humans. But they worked secretly to spread more pods until they could replace the entire human race. It was cool.

"Anybody who lives in a pod *has* to be an alien," I said.

"My mom says we should accept people

no matter where they live," Emily said.

"Your mom is weird," I told her.

"Maybe he's building a transmitter in there to contact his home planet," said Ryan. "Like in *E.T.*"

"Give it a rest with *E.T.*, will you?" I told Ryan.

Mr. Granite opened a door and went inside the pod thing. We all snuck up to it, like we were secret agents. It was cool. Andrea took a little camera out of her backpack.

"I'll bet he's taking off his human mask in there," Michael whispered.

"I'll snap the picture when he peels off his face," Andrea whispered.

"That will be a real Kodak moment," I whispered.

"I'm scared!" whispered Emily. "Maybe we should—"

But she never got the chance to finish her sentence. Because at that very second, Mr. Granite popped out of the pod!

"EEEEEEEEEEEKKKKKKKKK!" we all screamed.

"G'day, mates!" Mr. Granite said. He looked completely normal. "What can I do for you blokes?"

"Uh," I said, "we were just wondering if you trim your nose hair."

"You followed me home to ask if I trim my nose hair?" asked Mr. Granite.

"Well, actually, we wanted to know where you were born," said Andrea.

"I came from Neptune," said Mr. Granite.

"WOW," we all said, which is "MOM" upside down. So it was true! Mr. Granite really *IS* from another planet!

"Yes," he continued, "Neptune, New Jersey. Then my parents moved to Australia."

Oh.

Tattletales

I didn't believe for a minute that Mr. Granite was born in New Jersey. He was an alien from another planet for sure. And even though we didn't have a picture of him peeling off his face, we decided there was only one thing left for us to do: We had to tell Mr. Klutz.

The next morning we all met at school early to go to Mr. Klutz's office. When we got there, he was wearing one of those weird square hats we had to wear at graduation. And he was sticking his head out the window.

"Why are you sticking your head out the window?" Ryan asked.

"Oh, excuse me," said Mr. Klutz, pulling his head back inside. "I had to sharpen my pencil."

"You have a pencil sharpener outside your window?" asked Michael.

"No, I was just gathering solar energy to power my pencil sharpener," Mr. Klutz told us. "See? This cap has a solar panel in it. It was Mr. Granite's idea."

Mr. Klutz showed us how to sharpen a pencil with his solar-powered pencil sharpener. It was cool.

"We wanted to talk to you about Mr. Granite," said Ryan.

"I'm all ears," Mr. Klutz said.

"You are not," I told him. "You have eyes and a nose and a mouth, too. It would be

weird to be all ears."

"It's just an expression, dumbhead," said Andrea, rolling her eyes. "It means Mr. Klutz is listening."

"I knew that," I lied. "Anyway, we think there's something weird about Mr. Granite."

"Yes, I agree," Mr. Klutz said. "I can't put my finger on it."

"Why would you want to put your finger on it?" I asked.

"Mr. Granite lives in a pod," Emily said.

"And he has no nose hair," said Michael.

"Mr. Klutz," said Andrea, "we suspect that Mr. Granite is from another planet."

"Hmmmm," said Mr. Klutz. "It's funny you should mention that. The other day I saw a flying saucer in the teachers' lounge."

"WHAT?!" we all shouted. "You *did*?"

"Yes," said Mr. Klutz, "the teachers were throwing their teacups around again. I'll have to make another announcement about that."

"If Mr. Granite *is* an alien, will you have to fire him?" asked Emily.

"Or attack him with laser beams?" asked Ryan.

"Hmmmm," said Mr. Klutz.* "This has never come up before. I'm not sure aliens from other planets are allowed to teach third grade. I'll have to check in the Board

---

*Grown-ups always say "Hmmmm" when they're thinking. Nobody knows why.

of Education rule book."

"I'm bored of education," I said.

"In the meantime," said Mr. Klutz, "let's all keep our eyes peeled."

"That will probably hurt," I told him. "Can't we just watch Mr. Granite instead?"

"Okay, let's do that," he said. "I want to know everything about him. I want to know what makes him tick."

"Mr. Granite ticks?" I asked. "Maybe there's a clock inside him. Like the crocodile in *Peter Pan*."

"Maybe there's a *bomb* inside him!" Ryan said.

"Mr. Granite swallowed a bomb?" asked Emily. "We've got to *do* something!"

tick

tick tick

"Run for your lives!" shouted Neil the nude kid.

And we all went running out of Mr. Klutz's office.

The Truth About Mr. Granite

As it turned out, Mr. Granite didn't have a clock *or* a bomb inside him. I didn't even hear him tick. That day was a perfectly normal day. Or as normal as it can be when your teacher is from another planet.

When the three-o'clock bell rang, Mr.

Klutz made an announcement over the intercom.

"Have a great weekend, everyone," he said. "Next week we'll find out if Ella Mentry School is the greenest school in the county. I can almost taste that chocolate cake now! Oh, and teachers, please stop throwing teacups around the teachers' lounge. Thank you."

Me, Michael, and Ryan rode our bikes home. We were pretty tired, because we had been riding our bikes all day in class. But that's when I got the greatest idea in the history of the world!

"Hey," I told the guys, "I know how we can make our school the greenest school

71

in the county."

"How?" they asked.

"Let's paint it green!"

"A.J.," Ryan said, "you're a genius!"

"That's why I'm in the gifted and talented program," I said modestly. Everybody agreed that I should get the No Bell Prize.

That night, after dinner, I told my mom there was a bingo game at school. Michael and Ryan made up other excuses. Michael brought a bucket of green paint he found in his basement. Ryan brought some paintbrushes. We rode our bikes and met at the school.

"Okay," I told the guys, "let's start by painting the front door."

Michael opened up the paint can. Ryan gave me a brush. I was about to dip the brush into the paint when the most amazing thing in the history of the world happened. A guy jumped out from behind the bushes!

"Freeze, dirtbags!" he shouted.

AHHHHHHHH!

It was Officer Spence, the school security guard! He was supposed to protect the school from bad guys and criminals, not from *us*!

"Let's get out of here!" shouted Michael.

We hopped on our bikes and pedaled as fast as we could down the street. I never

even turned around to see if Officer Spence was chasing us.

"Whew! That was a close one!" Ryan said when we were a few blocks away from school.

"I don't think Officer Spence saw our faces," said Michael.

"Let's go home," I said.

Just as we were about to turn the corner, I realized something. This was Mr. Granite's street!

"Let's go over to Mr. Granite's house!"

I suggested. "Maybe we can catch him taking his face off."

We pedaled over to Mr. Granite's house. It was easy to find because of that giant POD thing on the grass. There was a light on inside the garage. We parked our bikes across the street and tiptoed over to the garage like secret agents. It was cool.

"Shhhhhh!" Ryan whispered. "Nobody scream if he peels off his face."

We peeked between the cracks in the garage door.

"Do you see anything?" Michael whispered.

"Look!" Ryan whispered back. "Mr. Granite is in there!"

"Yeah, over on the left," I whispered.

"What's he doing?" Ryan whispered.

"He's building something," Michael whispered.

And you'll never believe in a million hundred years what we saw Mr. Granite building in there.

I'm not gonna tell you.

Okay, okay, I'll tell you.

But you have to read the next chapter to find out. So nah-nah-nah boo-boo on you!

My Teacher
Is an Alien

Mr. Granite was building a *spaceship*!

It was red and black and silver, and it looked just like the spaceships you see in movies. It was cool!

"Andrea was *right*!" I whispered. "Mr. Granite *is* from another—"

But I never got the chance to finish my

sentence because at that moment, the garage door started going up. Mr. Granite, the alien, was standing there looking right at us!

I didn't know what to say! I didn't know what to do! I had to think fast!

"Freeze, dirtbag!" I yelled. "You're an alien, and we know it!"

Mr. Granite put his hands in the air. Then he realized we didn't have a gun or anything, so he put them down.

"Yes, I admit it," he said sadly. "I'm not from New Jersey. I'm from the planet Etinarg in a galaxy far, far away."

"WOW!" we all said, which is "MOM" upside down.

"Etinarg?" I said. "Isn't that 'Granite' spelled backward?"

"Yes," Mr. Granite said. "Everyone on Etinarg is named Granite."

"Doesn't it make things confusing when everybody has the same name?" asked Ryan.

"It does," Mr. Granite replied. "I was sent to Earth to help you stop global warming and to come back with some new names for our people. Now my work here is done. I must return to Etinarg. My spaceship is finished. I just need some rocket fuel so I can blast off."

"Wait a minute!" Michael said. "How do we know you're not yanking our chain? Prove you're an alien!"

"Yeah," I said. "Let's see you peel off your face."

"Well . . . okay," Mr. Granite said as he

put his hand under his chin.

I covered my eyes with my hands. I wanted to see Mr. Granite peel off his face; but at the same time, I didn't want to see what was underneath. What if it was scary? So I covered my eyes, but I opened my fingers so I could look between them.

Mr. Granite pulled at his neck, and the skin started to come loose. Then he peeled off his entire face! And you'll never believe in a million hundred years what he looked like underneath.

He looked exactly the same!

"Hey!" Ryan said. "That face looks just like the one you peeled off!"

"It never hurts to have an extra face,"

said Mr. Granite.

Even though Mr. Granite's peeled-off face looked the same as his regular face, it was still cool.

"Don't tell Mr. Klutz!" Mr. Granite said.

"Our lips are sealed," I told him. But not with glue. That would be weird.

Sad, Sad News

I couldn't sleep that night. All I could do was think about Mr. Granite. What if he was lying? What if he really came here to take over our planet and turn us into killer zombie robot slaves? Stuff like that happens all the time, you know. I wished I had been able to buy one of those laser beam pens at Staples.

Maybe Mr. Granite was just pretending

to be nice so it would be easier for him to

take over the world. Maybe I should tell Mr. Klutz. If I didn't say anything and Mr. Granite took over our planet, it would be all my fault.

This was the hardest decision I ever had to make. My brain hurt from thinking so much. I was afraid my head was gonna explode.

"Did you finish your homework?" my mom asked me on Monday morning.

"Homework?" I said. "Aliens from another planet could be attacking at this very second, and *you're* worried about *homework?"*

Finally, I decided to tell Mr. Klutz what I knew. As soon as I got to school, I marched into his office. He had a machine on his desk. It looked like a little microwave oven.

"Hey, check this out, A.J.!" said Mr. Klutz. "It's called the Ultimate Recycler. This gizmo can turn a can into a bottle, or a bottle into a can. So instead of throwing away a bottle, you just turn it into a can. And instead of throwing away a can, you just turn it into a bottle. This will be great for the environment!"

"Why not just take the can or bottle and rinse it out?" I asked. "Then you can use it again."

"Hmmmm," said Mr. Klutz. "That's a good idea, A.J. No wonder you're in the gifted and talented program."

He picked up the Ultimate Recycler and threw it into the recycling bin.

"Mr. Klutz," I said, "I have proof that Mr. Granite is from another planet. I saw him building a spaceship in his garage."

"Hmmmmm," Mr. Klutz said. "Well, I have some news for you, A.J. I looked through the Board of Education rule book very carefully, and there is nothing in there that says aliens from other planets can't teach third grade."

"So Mr. Granite can stay on Earth if he wants to?"

"That's right," said Mr. Klutz. "In fact, I'll call him in here right now to tell him the good news."

Mr. Klutz called Mr. Granite on the intercom. A few minutes later, Mr. Granite came into the office. When he saw me, he looked mad.

"It's okay," Mr. Klutz told Mr. Granite. "I know you're from another planet. But I think you're an excellent teacher, and I want you to stay at Ella Mentry School."

Mr. Klutz and Mr. Granite hugged, which was weird.

"You are very kind," Mr. Granite said. "But my work here is done. I am ready to return to my home planet of Etinarg. I blast off Friday."

"But I thought you said you didn't have any rocket fuel," I said.

"I don't need rocket fuel anymore," Mr. Granite told me. "I met with Mr. Docker over the weekend, and he figured out a way to power my spaceship with potatoes."

Wow! I knew you could power a car with potatoes. And I knew you could power a computer with potatoes. But how are you going to get a spaceship off the ground with just potato power?

"Is that possible?" I asked.

"It is," Mr. Granite said. "We're going to microwave the potatoes."

Saying Good-bye to Mr. Granite

At three o'clock on Friday, the school secretary, Mrs. Patty, made an announcement that everybody had to go to the all-purpose room. When we got there, Mr. Klutz was up on the stage. He was holding a piece of paper.

"I have big news!" Mr. Klutz told us.

"Mr. Klutz has a big nose," I whispered to Ryan.

"Are we the greenest school in the county?" asked Neil the nude kid.

"No, we came in second place," Mr. Klutz said.

Everybody groaned because that meant we weren't going to have a chocolate cake party.

"Second place?" Michael asked. "How could *any* school be greener than ours?"

"Well," said Mr. Klutz, "the students at one of the other schools actually painted their school green! Too bad *we* didn't think of that."

I looked at Ryan. Ryan looked at Michael.

Michael looked at me.

"So what's the big news?" asked Neil the nude kid.

"The big news is that we received a letter from the president of the United States!" said Mr. Klutz.

"WOW!" we all said, which is "MOM" upside down. I stuck my tongue out at Andrea, because she had thought it was a dumb idea to write to the president.

Mr. Klutz read the letter:

Dear Students of Ella Mentry School,

Thank you for the nice letter. I just wanted to let you know that I do not have a nose attached to my foot.

Sincerely,
The President

It was cool to get a letter from the president, even if the letter made no sense at all.

"I have more big news," Mr. Klutz told us. "Our third-grade teacher, Mr. Granite, is from a planet called Etinarg; and he is going home today. So we're going to have a going-away party . . . with chocolate cake!"

"YAY!" everybody yelled.

We went out to the playground, where there was the biggest chocolate cake in the history of the world. Everybody was out there, even Jackie Macky. Mr. Brad cut

the cake and Mrs. Jafee passed out pieces
to everybody. Mr. Granite's spaceship was
out in the field, near the cows. It was covered with potatoes.

"MOOOOOOOO,"
said a cow.

We stuffed our faces with so much cake, I thought I was gonna throw up. It was the greatest day of my life. After we finished, Mr. Granite put on a space suit, and we went over to say good-bye to him. It was really sad.

"I'm going to miss you kids," said Mr. Granite. "When I get home, I'm going to name my Etinarg friends A.J., Andrea, Ryan, Emily, Michael, and Neil."

"We'll miss you too," said Andrea.

"I hope that after I am gone," Mr. Granite told us, "you will keep saving energy and living green."

"We will!" we all shouted.

Everybody was sad to see Mr. Granite

go. Emily cried, of course. So did some of the teachers. Mr. Granite waved to us as he climbed into his spaceship. Everybody gathered around. Mrs. Yonkers went over to her computer and announced the countdown.

"10 . . . 9 . . . 8 . . . 7 . . . 6 . . . 5 . . . 4 . . . 3 . . . 2 . . . 1!" said Mrs. Yonkers. "Begin microwaving the potatoes!"

Our science teacher, Mr. Docker, flipped a switch. Nothing happened for like a million hundred seconds. Then there was a little *ding* sound. Steam started pouring out of the potatoes. The whole field smelled like baked potatoes. Slowly, the spaceship began rising off the ground.

"LIFT-OFF!" yelled Mrs. Yonkers. "We have liftoff!"

That's when the most amazing thing in the history of the world happened. One of the cows must have liked the smell of baked potatoes, because it came running over to the spaceship.

The cow bumped right into it!

The spaceship was going up crooked!

"Houston, we have a problem!" shouted Mr. Docker.

The spaceship zoomed to the left. Then it zoomed to the right. It was zigzagging back and forth in the sky over the school.

"Abandon ship!" shouted Mrs. Yonkers. "Abandon ship!"

The door to the spaceship opened, and Mr. Granite jumped out. A parachute opened, and he floated back down to Earth.

Well, he *almost* floated back down to

Earth. On the way down,
his parachute landed on
the windmill.

The ropes got all tan-
gled up!

Mr. Granite was caught on the windmill!

He was spinning around and around!

It was a real Kodak moment. You should have been there.

Meanwhile, Mr. Granite's spaceship crash-landed in a field across the street from our school. It exploded! Pieces of baked potato went flying everywhere! It was cool. And we got to see it live and in person.

Well, that's pretty much the way it all went down. The windmill finally stopped turning, and the teachers were able to get Mr. Granite back on the ground again.

Maybe Mr. Granite will build another spaceship. Or maybe he'll just stay on Earth and be our teacher. Maybe Andrea will stop recycling her toilet paper and put her head in a paper shredder. Maybe there won't be any more flying saucers in the teachers' lounge. Maybe Jackie Macky will stop sucking her own toes. Maybe the president will trim the hair on the nose attached to his foot. Maybe Ryan will stop talking about E.T. Maybe they'll start selling laser beam pens at Staples. Maybe the sun will explode. Maybe Emily will stop running into cows. Maybe we'll find out what makes Mr. Granite tick. Maybe we'll be able to hear words like "naked" and

"Uranus" without giggling.

But it won't be easy!*

---

*This story is supposed to be funny, but *all* of us should live green. To find out more, go to

• EPA Global Warming Kids Site (www.epa.gov/global-warming/kids)

• The Green Squad (www.nrdc.org/greensquad)

• Minnesota Pollution Control Agency Kids Page (www.pca.state.mn.us/kids)

• Environmental Kids Club (www.epa.gov/kids)

• Earth Day in Your Neighborhood (www.allspecies.org/neigh/blocka.htm)

• Tree Musketeers (www.treemusketeers.org)

• United States Environmental Protection Agency (http://epa.gov/climatechange/wycd/waste/kids.html)

Check out the My Weird School series!

#1: Miss Daisy Is Crazy!

The first book in the hilarious series stars A.J., a second grader who hates school—and can't believe his teacher hates it too!

#2: Mr. Klutz Is Nuts!

A.J. can't believe his crazy principal wants to climb to the top of the flagpole!

#3: Mrs. Roopy Is Loopy!

The new librarian thinks she's George Washington one day and Little Bo Peep the next!

#4: Ms. Hannah Is Bananas!

The art teacher wears clothes made from pot holders. Worse than that, she's trying to make A.J. be partners with yucky Andrea!

#5: Miss Small Is off the Wall!

The gym teacher is teaching A.J.'s class to juggle scarves, balance feathers, and do everything *but* play sports!

#6: Mr. Hynde Is Out of His Mind!

The music teacher plays bongo drums on the principal's bald head! But does he have what it takes to be a real rock-and-roll star?

#7: Mrs. Cooney Is Loony!

The school nurse is everybody's favorite—but is she hiding a secret identity?

#8: Ms. LaGrange Is Strange!

The new lunch lady talks funny—and why is she writing secret messages in the mashed potatoes?

#9: Miss Lazar Is Bizarre!

What kind of grown-up *likes* cleaning throw-up? Miss Lazar is the weirdest custodian in the world!

#10: Mr. Docker Is off His Rocker!

The science teacher alarms and amuses A.J.'s class with his wacky experiments and nutty inventions.